MEET THE GIRL TALK CHARACTERS

Sabrina Wells is petite, with curly auburn hair, sparkling hazel eyes, and a bubbly personality. Sabrina loves magazines, shopping, sleepovers, and most of all, she loves talking to her best friends.

Katie Campbell is a straight-A student and super athlete. With her blond hair, blue eyes, and matching clothes, she's everyone's idea of Little Miss Perfect. But Katie has a few surprises for everyone, including herself!

Randy Zak has just moved to Acorn Falls from New York City, and is she ever cool! With her radical spiked haircut and her hip New York clothes, Randy teaches everyone just how much fun it is to be different.

Allison Cloud is a Native American Indian. Allison's supersmart and really beautiful. But she has one major problem: She's thirteen years old, five foot seven, and still growing!

Sara Crawford

RANDY AND THE GREAT CANOE RACE

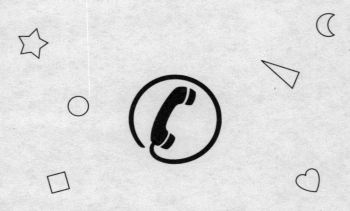

By L. E. Blair

GIRL TALK® series created by Western Publishing Company, Inc.

Western Publishing Company, Inc., Racine, Wisconsin 53404

R MCMXCIII

Text by Katherine Applegate

Chapter One

"'Question number one,'" Sabrina Wells announced, reading aloud from a copy of *Young Chic* magazine. It was Saturday evening and we were having a sleepover at Sabs's house. "'Would you describe yourself as: A, sultry and mysterious; B, strong and forceful; C, perky and upbeat; or D, withdrawn and distant?'" She paused and flopped onto her bed. "Knowing myself the way I do, I'd have to say A."

"*A?*" I asked incredulously.

"A?" Katie echoed. "*You?* Sultry and mysterious?"

"I am *very* mysterious," Sabrina replied. She pulled a lock of her curly red hair over her left eye and wiggled her eyebrows suggestively. "In fact, I'm *so* mysterious, you don't even realize I'm mysterious."

I had to laugh. Of the four of us in the room — Sabs, Allison Cloud, Katie Campbell, and me, Randy Zak — Sabrina was the *last* person you'd ever think of as being mysterious.

"You know it's C," I said. "If you're not perky and upbeat, I don't know who is."

"I suppose you're right, Randy," Sabs replied, pouting, "but I don't want to be a C my whole life. I want to be an A. Or at least a B."

"Allison's an A," Katie said. "It's that Native American heritage. It gives her that mysterious and sultry look. Even when she's just spacing out — reading a book and ignoring her friends." She gave Allison a sidelong look and then winked at me.

"I am *not* spacing out," Allie said without looking up from her book. "I heard everything you guys said."

"What *are* you reading?" I asked, craning my neck so I could see the book's cover. "Social studies? You're actually doing social studies homework on a Saturday evening while we're supposed to be hanging out?"

Allie set the book down with a sigh. "I just had to finish this chapter. Once I got started, I couldn't put it down."

That's typical Allison. She loves to read. Last summer, just for fun, she read a hundred books. But Allie is far from being a nerd. In fact, she's one of the coolest people I know.

"Hey, social studies can wait," I teased. "We have more important things to figure out. Sabs's quiz will answer the burning question 'Do You See Yourself as Others See You?'"

"'Question number two,'" Sabs continued, now that she had Al's full attention. "'Would you describe your personal style as: A, simple and practical; B, outrageous and avant-garde; C, preppie and conservative; or D, cute and sparkly?'"

"That's easy," Al said. "Each of us fits one of those descriptions perfectly."

"And I'm the outrageous and avant-garde one, right?" Sabs demanded with a mock-threatening look.

Al laughed. "Sorry, Sabs. I think that's Randy's territory."

I looked down at my black spandex mini-skirt, purple leggings, silver-buckled black boots, and studded denim jacket. "Me? Outrageous and avant-garde? Maybe in Acorn Falls, but back in New York —"

"Look out!" Katie interrupted. "Randy's having another New York Attack!"

"I am *not*," I protested. "But back in New York this outfit —"

Suddenly all three of them began singing that song "New York, New York" at the top of their lungs. You know — that famous song about New York City.

I guess they're a little tired of listening to me compare Acorn Falls to New York City. See, my mom and I moved to Acorn Falls, Minnesota, after she and my dad got divorced. She grew up around here, and she thought it would be a good place for me to grow up, too.

Everything was so different from what I was used to back East, I really had trouble getting used to the place. I really like it here now. But that doesn't mean I can't complain a *little* now and then, just to keep in practice.

"Okay, okay," I said, holding up my hands in surrender. "I got the message! Just stop that horrible singing — *please!*"

They all stopped instantly and gave each other high-fives.

"You're all very funny," I said sarcastically. "Not!"

"As I was saying before that unfortunate New York Attack," Al continued, "that quiz has

4

each of us down just about right. I dress in a simple and practical style" — it's true that Al isn't into clothes much, but what she'd neglected to add was that she looks *great* in anything — "and Randy is outrageous and avant-garde."

"Whatever *that* means," Sabs added.

"And, of course, let's face it," Al went on, "Katie is the preppie of the group."

Katie stood up and twirled around, showing off her perfectly matched khaki shorts and argyle sweater, which *also* matched her sky-blue socks and headband. "I strive for a classic style," she said in a fake-snooty voice. "Conservative, yet alluring."

"And that just leaves —"

"Don't say it," Sabs warned. "I am *not* cute and sparkly!"

"Okay," I quickly agreed. "You are *not* cute and sparkly."

Sabs looked at me suspiciously. "How come you're agreeing so easily?"

I sniffed the air. "Because the Zak junk food radar system has just informed me that your mom is baking chocolate-chip cookies."

All four of us leaped to our feet. Mrs. Wells can definitely bake cookies. In fact, she can cook *anything*, unlike my mom, who finds making cold cereal a challenge.

M (that's what I call my mom) may not be much of a cook, but she's an incredible artist, and I wouldn't have her trade that for anything — even cooking talent. Besides, I can always hang out at Sabs's house when I need a fresh-baked cookie fix.

We piled down the two flights of stairs that lead from Sabs's room — which is in the attic — down to the Wellses' big, old-fashioned kitchen. As I predicted, Mrs. Wells was just taking a pan of golden-brown scrumptious-looking cookies out of the oven. Using a metal spatula, she slipped the cookies off the pan and onto a big platter on the kitchen table.

"Help yourselves, girls," Mrs. Wells said with a smile when she spotted us hovering in the doorway.

We headed straight for the platter like four chocolate chip–seeking missiles. But suddenly, just as we were closing in on the cookies, Sabs's twin brother, Sam, appeared, along with three of his friends.

"Cookies!" Sam yelled. "Get 'em, boys, before Blabs and her friends scarf them all up!"

In the next half-second, we girls dived on the cookies. Unfortunately, so did all four guys. It was not a pretty sight — sixteen hands trying to snatch up as many steaming-hot cookies as possible. It was hard to tell which side won, because all we ended up holding were handfuls of crumbs and gooey chocolate chips.

"Kids!" Mrs. Wells yelled in dismay. "There are plenty more cookies on the way. There's no need to go wild."

"Oh, it's okay, Mom," Sam said with a grin. "It's no problem. We *like* going wild."

"Well, all of you out of my kitchen. I don't want to be trampled to death when I pull out the next batch!"

She made shooing gestures, and we all piled into the living room, gobbling up the hot, drippy cookies.

"We saw those cookies first," Sabs complained to her brother. It's kind of hard to tell sometimes, but Sabs and Sam really are close.

"Hey, it's the law of the jungle," Sam said. "Only the strong survive."

"More like 'only the greedy,'" Katie shot back.

"Look, we're men," said Greg Loggins, who's

one of Sam's friends. He shrugged. "We need more food than you girls."

"Men? You'll be men in about ten years — maybe!" I countered.

"Very funny," Greg said. He gave me a dirty look, then gulped down a chunk of cookie dripping with chocolate. "But while you girls were sitting around here painting your toenails, or whatever it is you do, *we* were out on the river with my dad canoeing." He rolled up his sleeve and flexed his right arm to show off his muscles. "You need a lot of food to build this kind of power."

My friends and I all broke up laughing. He looked like such a dweeb, standing there showing off. But Katie marched up to him and calmly rolled up *her* sleeve. Then she flexed her muscle.

Maybe I should explain. In some ways Katie seems like a totally perfect preppie, with perfect long blond hair and perfect grades and perfectly matched outfits. But Katie's also on the hockey team — the *boys'* hockey team — and here in Minnesota they take hockey very, very seriously. They play rough, and Katie doesn't get any special treatment because she's a girl.

The boys looked from Greg's muscle to Katie's, then back again. You could tell from their shocked expressions that Katie had won the Battle of the Biceps.

"Big deal," Jason McKee said at last. "Greg is still a guy. And guy muscles have more endurance."

"Oh, puh-leeze," Al put in.

"It's true," Greg said. He rolled down his sleeve, eyeing Katie suspiciously. "We paddled for four hours straight down the river. Then after lunch we paddled two hours more."

I laughed. "Like we couldn't do that, too?"

"There's no way," Sam said. "I mean, look at you girls. Maybe Katie here can swing a hockey stick when she has to, but I happen to know that Blabs can barely open a jar of pickles."

"The top was stuck!" Sabs said hotly.

"And all Allison ever does is turn the pages of a book. And as for you, Zak," Sam sneered, "just because you can play drums and like to skateboard, that doesn't make you a he-man like us." He struck a pose like a bodybuilder, and Greg, Jason, and Nick Robbins followed suit, grunting and flexing their muscles like a bunch of miniature Arnold Schwarzeneggers.

"I don't need to be a he-man," I said. "I can be a she-woman!"

But the guys just laughed as they headed off, still doing their exaggerated bodybuilder moves.

"You think you guys are so tough?" I called. "How about a little contest?" It wasn't exactly like I *meant* to say it. It just popped out. I can't always rely on my mouth to behave.

The guys all stopped dead in their tracks. "Excuse me," Greg said, spinning around. "Did you just say something about a contest?"

Nick nodded. "I do believe I heard something about a contest."

"I doubt Randy meant it," Sam said, smirking. "She probably just blurted it out without thinking. You know how silly girls are."

How could I ignore that? "You think you guys are so tough?" I cried. "Fine. We challenge you to . . . to a canoe race!"

Out of the corner of my eye, I could see Al looking at me with a mixture of shock and horror. Sabs was standing off to one side, shaking her head and silently mouthing the word *no*. But it was a little late to back down now.

"Time and place, Zak?" Sam said, grinning confidently.

"I'll get back to you," I said quickly. Then, mustering as much swagger as I could, I headed back upstairs, with my friends close behind.

"Can you believe those guys?" I asked when we were all back in Sabs's room. "I haven't heard that much grunting since I went to the ape house at the zoo!"

"You know," Al said, "you really could have consulted us before making that bet, Ran."

"You mean, those gorillas weren't getting on your nerves?" I demanded.

"Hey, watch it, Randy!" Sabs interjected, holding up a warning finger.

"Sorry, Sabs," I said, thinking that she was about to stick up for Sam.

"I should hope you are," Sabs replied, sniffing. "Gorillas are actually very intelligent, civilized animals!"

I laughed. "Well, in any case, I'm sorry I didn't check it out with all of you before opening my mouth. But you know how those guys are. By tomorrow they'll have forgotten all about that bet."

The more I thought about it over the weekend, the more I was sure that there was no way Sam and his friends had taken me seriously. I mean, hey, I'm just not a water sports kind of person, unless you count dancing in the shower.

Anyway, I figured, no big deal. Those guys have the attention span of houseplants. There was no way they'd even remember my little challenge.

At least that's what I thought. That's what Sabs, Katie, and Al thought, too.

Until we got to the lunchroom on Monday.

"Excuse me, excuse me! May I have your attention!" someone shouted out as soon as we sat down and started to eat.

We all looked up from our lunches to see Sam standing on a chair in the middle of the lunchroom.

"Oh, no," Sabs moaned.

"Fellow students of Bradley Junior High!" Sam shouted as the room grew quiet. "I have an announcement. On Saturday a certain girl, who shall remain nameless — but let's just say she usually dresses in black, plays drums, and comes from New York . . ."

Of course, every single person in the room turned toward me.

". . . a certain girl and her friends challenged me and my friends to a canoe race. Men against girls."

I stood up. "I think you mean *women* against *boys*!"

This drew a few cheers — mostly from girls. And a few boos — mostly from boys.

"I propose we hold this race three weekends from now," Sam said, still standing on his chair. "That'll give you girls plenty of time to prepare . . . so you can *lose*, fair and square."

I looked at Sabs, who sent back a "Why me?" look. Then I glanced at Al, who just looked a little sick. Even Katie looked a little worried. And, of course, I knew I was terrified.

So, naturally, I did the only thing I possibly could. I pointed my finger at Sam and announced, "We'll be there, and we'll teach you guys a lesson you won't forget!"

Chapter Two

Sabs calls Randy.

RANDY: Zak residence.

SABRINA: Randy? This is Sabrina.

RANDY: Hey, Sabs. What's up?

SABRINA: Not very much, really, except that when I got home from school today, Sam started in on me about this whole canoe thing.

RANDY: What do you mean, "started in on" you?

SABRINA: You know — teasing me. I'm used to that. But he was going on and on about how we don't know anything about canoeing, and how he and the other guys have all kinds of experience. He even said Greg's dad is a champion canoer or something.

RANDY: (*Pauses*) So, what did you say?

14

SABRINA: Well, I started to argue with him. But then it sort of hit me.

RANDY: What sort of hit you?

SABRINA: That maybe Sam is right. I mean, what do we know about canoeing?

RANDY: What's there to know? Canoe, paddles, water. It's not exactly brain surgery, Sabs.

SABRINA: That's what he said you'd say.

RANDY: Who?

SABRINA: Sam. He said I should ask if you had any experience canoeing. Then he said you'd probably say something like "Hey, it isn't exactly rocket science." Only instead of saying "rocket science," you said "brain surgery."

RANDY: Come on, Sabs. Are you really going to let Sam's he-man act get to you?

SABRINA: Um, not exactly. But you know how Sam is — if he finds something to tease me about, he makes my life unbearable!

RANDY: Just think how unbearable he'll be

if we don't go through with the race.

SABRINA: Yeah, I guess you're right. If we back out now, I'll have to hear about it for the rest of my life. I just hope we win.

RANDY: Of course we'll win. I have total, absolute confidence.

SABRINA: Good, because Sam and I made this bet. If his team wins, I have to do all his chores for a week.

RANDY: A whole week?

SABRINA: Uh-oh! Now you sound like you think we're going to lose!

RANDY: I was only asking a question. That's all. Listen, no way are we going to lose against those guys. We have to go into this thing with confidence. We have to believe in ourselves! If you believe you can win, then you can!

SABRINA: You're right!

RANDY: Have faith! Realize you can do anything!

SABRINA: Yeah! You are so right!

RANDY: And as you're out on that river, paddling toward victory, just remember one thing.

SABRINA: What's that?

RANDY: If we lose that race, Sam will tease you about it for the rest of your life.

SABRINA: Thanks, Ran. I really needed that little reminder.

RANDY: Hey, what are friends for?

SABRINA: I've got to get off now. Bye.

RANDY: *Ciao.*

Randy calls Allison.

ALLISON: Hello? Cloud residence.

RANDY: Hey, Al, it's me, Randy.

ALLISON: Hi, Randy. What's going on?

RANDY: I just got a call from Sabs. Sam is really getting to her. I think she's losing faith in our ability to win this canoe race.

ALLISON: (*Laughing*) You mean, she actually had some faith to lose?

RANDY: You, too? Don't you think we can win?

ALLISON: I'm just being logical. The boys' team is bigger than we are, stronger than we are, and more experienced than we are.

RANDY: So, why did you back me up when I challenged them?

ALLISON: Hey, you're my best friend. You'd back me up if I just blurted out some wild bet, wouldn't you?

RANDY: I didn't just blurt it out. (*Pauses*) Okay, maybe I blurted a *little*, but those guys really need somebody to teach them a lesson.

ALLISON: But how can we teach them a lesson about canoeing when none of us knows the first thing about it?

RANDY: So you've never been canoeing, either, I guess. (*Sighs*) So, what we're saying is you don't know how to paddle a canoe, Sabs doesn't know how to paddle a canoe, and I don't know how to paddle a canoe. How about Katie?

ALLISON: I asked her. She said she was pretty sure that *you* knew how to handle a canoe.

RANDY: Me?

ALLISON: She said there was no way you'd

take on a bet unless you had a
good reason to think you could
win.

RANDY: Oh. (*Long pause*) Well, I'd better
get going. I have a lot of planning
to do.

ALLISON: What planning?

RANDY: I have to plan how I can sneak out
of town before this race.

ALLISON: Don't give up hope.

RANDY: I'll send you a letter when I get far
enough away. *Ciao.*

ALLISON: Bye.

Katie calls Randy.

RANDY: Speak to me.

KATIE: Hi, this is Katie. I've been trying
to, but your phone's been busy for
ages.

RANDY: I was talking to Al and Sabs. They
don't think we have a prayer of
winning this canoe race.

KATIE: Well, you've canoed before, right?
What do you think?

RANDY: Me? I think we should all split
town and assume new identities.

KATIE: Randy . . . are you telling me you
           don't know anything about canoe-
           ing?

RANDY: Why does everyone keep thinking
           that I'm some major league canoe
           expert?

KATIE: I'm just going to take a wild guess
           on this, but maybe because you're
           the one who came up with the
           idea for this race?

RANDY: (*Clears her throat*) Look, Katie, the
           only boat I've ever been on is the
           Staten Island Ferry, back when I
           was living in New York.

KATIE: I wish I'd known this before I bet
           my stepbrother two weeks' allow-
           ance that we'd blow Sam and those
           guys out of the water.

RANDY: You bet Michel two whole weeks'
           allowance? Are you insane? That's
           even worse than Sabs's bet.

KATIE: Uh-oh. Did she bet her allowance?

RANDY: Worse. She bet Sam a whole week
           of chores. (*Randy groans.*) You're
           all going to hate me by the time
           this race is over. Assuming, that

	is, we don't all drown first.
KATIE:	At least we all know how to swim. That's something.
RANDY:	It should come in very handy when we capsize the canoe.
KATIE:	Come on, Randy. Those guys really made me mad, too, when they started saying how weak and klutzy girls are. I think the race was a great idea.
RANDY:	If we win it, you mean.
KATIE:	We can win. I know we can.
RANDY:	But none of us knows the first thing about canoeing.
KATIE:	So we'll find someone who does. And we'll practice our rears off for the next three weeks.
RANDY:	And?
KATIE:	(*Pauses*) And at least if we lose, we'll know that we didn't give up without a fight.
RANDY:	I know you're right. But help me convince Sabs and Al, okay?
KATIE:	Deal.
RANDY:	And Katie?
KATIE:	Yes?

RANDY: Promise me — no more bets. I won't be able to stand the guilt. *Ciao*.

KATIE: Bye.

Chapter Three

By Tuesday afternoon we still hadn't found anyone to help us. We needed someone to drive us to the river and help us rent the canoe. I couldn't help wondering how we were ever going to win when we couldn't even get to a boat to practice! I had tried to sound upbeat and confident with my friends all day at school. But my optimism was fading by the second.

I still hadn't mentioned anything about the Great Canoe Race to M. To tell the truth, I was still kind of hoping one of my friends would come up with a miracle, so we wouldn't have to race.

I wanted to tell M, and I wanted her to come to the race, too. But I couldn't help thinking that being humiliated in front of the whole school was going to be bad enough. Why be embarrassed in front of my mom, too?

Not exactly positive thinking, I guess.

We had decided to have a brainstorming meeting at my house right after school. I ran ahead to get some munchies and make sure M was okay about my friends coming over.

Katie was the first to show up at my house. M and I live in a big converted barn. Of course, looking at the inside, you'd never really guess that it used to be a hangout for cows. It looks fairly normal, except that it's basically one great big room, with skylights. I have the only really separate room. It's upstairs, in what used to be the hayloft. M's room and art studio are downstairs, past the kitchen and set apart by Chinese screens.

"So, how did it go?" I asked Katie as soon as I'd swung open the front door. "Did you find someone to drive us?"

She shook her head. "Nope. My mom and my stepdad are too busy to do it. I tried talking Princess Emily into it, but she has some concert she has to go to with her boyfriend. She wished us luck, though."

Princess Emily is Katie's nickname for her older sister. Katie thinks she's a real Miss Perfect. Of course, since Katie is sort of Miss

Perfect herself, it's kind of funny.

I sighed, sinking onto the couch. "Do you think Sabs will come up with anyone?"

"In about two seconds you can ask her," Katie replied, joining me. "I saw Sabs and Allison heading up the street from the other direction. They should be here right about —"

The doorbell rang and I went to answer it. Sure enough, there stood Al and Sabs. "Hi, guys. Did either of you have any luck finding someone to help with the canoe stuff?" I asked hopefully.

"Don't look at me," Sabs said. "I'm stuck with nothing but brothers, and they've all taken Sam's side." Sabs sighed and sat down cross-legged on the floor. "And as for my mom, well, she doesn't know anything about canoeing."

Like I said, Mrs. Wells is a great cook. But she isn't exactly the athletic type, and we were kind of hoping that whoever we got to help us could maybe coach us a little, too.

I looked questioningly at Al. She shrugged and shook her head. "Don't look at me."

"Great. So on top of not knowing anything about canoeing, we can't even find anyone to drive us to the river," Sabs complained.

"Hey, you guys promised me at lunch today that you were going to get psyched up for this," Katie said.

"Katie's right," I agreed. "If we're going to get blown away, we can at least go down with some dignity."

"Who's getting blown away?" M asked casually, stepping out of her studio to take a break from painting. From the stains on her smock, I felt pretty sure she was painting something very blue.

"Um, well —" I began.

"We need kind of a coach for a canoe race that we're having against a bunch of boys who are much more experienced than we are," Sabs said in a rush. "And we can't find anyone to help us."

"Well, why didn't you ask me?" M asked, sounding a tiny bit hurt. "Didn't you think I could do it?"

"It's not that, M," I said. "It's just that I didn't want to drag you into this dumb idea of mine. I was the one who challenged the guys, because they were acting all macho and superior."

"Yeah, she just wants to drag her three best

friends into this dumb idea of hers," Katie said, tossing a throw pillow at me.

"You girls sound like you've given up already," M chided.

"Well, logically speaking, we don't have much of a chance," Al pointed out. "The guys are stronger and more experienced than we are. Plus, they've got Greg's father as their coach. He knows an awful lot about the river, and about canoeing."

"He does, does he?" M said, rolling her eyes. "Well, he's not the only one." She smiled. "It just so happens that *I* was a star on Camp Winotonka's first-place canoe team," M announced proudly.

"You were?" I asked in surprise. This was definitely interesting news.

"I was," M said nonchalantly. "My team beat out every other camp on the lake for three summers in a row."

"Cool," Katie said. "We've finally found someone who actually knows how to work a canoe."

M laughed. "Hey, it's not exactly quantum physics."

"Or rocket science," Sabs said with a giggle.

"Or brain surgery," I added, laughing.

"So, will you help us, Olivia?" Sabs asked. M wants all my friends to call her by her first name, but Sabs is the only one who actually does.

"Of course I will," M said. "But the first thing we're going to have to do is get over this negative attitude you girls seem to have. You've got to believe we can win!"

"Couldn't I just believe in the Tooth Fairy?" I said, laughing. "It'd be a whole lot easier."

M gave me a warning look. "I'm *serious*. If we're going to do this, we have to go in with a winning attitude!"

"I suppose that, technically, almost anything is possible," Al mused.

"That's the spirit!" M said.

I was a little surprised. I've never exactly thought of M as the competitive type.

"And the second thing you'll do," M said, planting her hands on her hips, "is practice, practice, practice!"

"We will?" I said.

"Sure we will," Katie said enthusiastically, giving M a smile.

"Starting this Saturday," M added firmly.

She was sounding more like a real coach every second. It was absolutely amazing. "Believe me, after you learn some of the basics and get a little experience, you'll realize it *can* be done. After the first practice, you girls are going to realize that you can really win, if you set your minds to it!"

The following Saturday morning we were up bright and early. *Too* early, if you ask me.

M's no more of a morning person than I am, but you wouldn't have known that from the way she dragged me out of bed at the crack of dawn. We picked up Sabs, Katie, and Al and headed straight to the river, M giving us pep talks the whole way.

While M and Katie went over to the boat-house to rent our canoe, the rest of us flopped on some benches at picnic tables down by the water.

"I can't believe we're out here in the woods," I moaned. "At the crack of dawn on a perfectly good Saturday, no less."

"And we're about to jump into a canoe," Sabs added with a yawn.

"It *is* sort of crazy if you think of it logically,"

Al agreed.

I guess I was the last person who should have been complaining. But it was hard to have a pumped attitude when you were basically sleepwalking.

"Hey, guys, what are you doing? Taking a nap?" Katie called as she and M returned.

"Let's go," M said enthusiastically. "Brendan has our canoe ready for us."

"*Brendan?*" I echoed, raising an eyebrow.

M fluttered her eyelashes at me. "He runs the canoe-rental counter."

We trudged over to the little boathouse where about a dozen canoes and big inner-tube rubber rafts were stacked. A very cute dude with long blond hair and major muscles was setting a red canoe on the riverbank, with the back half in the water.

"Brendan?" I asked M.

She grinned. "See? I knew this would be fun."

"Okay, your paddles are already in the canoe," Brendan told us, "and it looks like you all need life jackets."

"Right, life jackets, everyone," M said firmly. "You're all to wear life jackets at all times."

Brendan passed them out, and we began trying to figure out how to put them on. Sabs finally gave up when hers wouldn't seem to stay on.

"Hold on a minute," Brendan said to Sabs. "I'll go get you a children's size."

Sabs buried her face in her hands. "Wonderful!" she moaned. "I'm already humiliated, and we haven't even started!"

A moment later Brendan came back from the shack with a life jacket that fit Sabs perfectly.

"Now, you want your most experienced people at the front and at the back," Brendan explained as we stood around the canoe, waiting to get in.

"M is our only experienced canoer," I said.

"Hey, I'm just the coach, remember?" she said. "I'll get in this time, but you four are going to be doing the actual paddling."

"Who's the strongest of you girls?" Brendan asked.

Slowly we all turned to look at Katie. "Time to show off those famous muscles again, Katie," I said.

"Okay," she agreed. "I'll steer." While Brendan held the boat steady, she got in and sat down at the front.

"Just a second, Katie," M said. "You steer a canoe from the back."

"Oh — okay," Katie replied. She got up, climbed to the rear, and sat down in the last seat. Then came M, then Sabs, then Al. I stationed myself in the front.

"All set?" Brendan called.

"Yes, I'll take it from here," M said. "Thanks, Brendan."

There were paddles in the bottom of the canoe, and at M's command we each grabbed hold of one.

While M told us how to use our paddles to push off from the riverbank, Brendan pushed at the front of the canoe. A few seconds later we were floating away from the shore.

"Good launch, girls," M said encouragingly. I looked up at M, thinking that our former Camp Winotonka champion was in for a wild ride.

"Remember — the first rest stop where you can dock the canoe is a mile downstream. Just look for our sign," Brendan called from the shore. "If you go past that one, there are other rest stops farther along. And if you get into any real trouble, there's a flare under the front seat. Just launch it and wait. We'll get to you eventually."

As the canoe bobbed along, we all looked down at our paddles with a mixture of curiosity and confusion. I stuck mine in the water and tried out a stroke. The canoe moved a slight distance through the water.

"Hey, it worked!" I said. "Cool."

Al and Sabs both followed my example, and instantly we were on our way.

Chapter Four

"This is easy," Sabs said happily as a few more strokes moved us out toward the current.

But at that very moment the swift-moving water grabbed us, snatching the front end of the canoe and spinning us around. I looked up and realized we were facing right back toward shore.

"Katie!" I yelled. "Aren't you supposed to be steering?"

"How can I steer if you don't make the boat go forward?" she grumbled.

"Okay, calm down, girls. Let's get organized here," M said in a very coachlike tone. "Randy, you and Sabs paddle on the left side. Al, you paddle on the right side. Katie, you take the right side, too, except when you need to steer."

"But we're pointed the wrong way," Sabs said nervously.

"I noticed that, Sabs," M said patiently.

"Okay, everyone paddle backward."

Al started to get up and turn around. The whole canoe began to wobble.

"No, Allison," M called. "Stay seated like you were. Just make your paddle go the other way. Put the paddle about half in and push the water away."

"Like this?" I asked, demonstrating what I thought would be the way to do it.

"Right. Not choppy," M said. "Try to get a long, smooth stroke." Then she demonstrated, waving her arms in the air a little like an orchestra conductor, which nearly made me crack up laughing.

We all gave it a shot, and sure enough, the canoe began to move backward. This time the current snatched the back of the boat and spun us around so we were facing in the right direction again.

"Nobody move!" I yelled. "If we go forward, the current will just spin us around backward again."

"So we're just going to sit here all day?" Katie demanded.

"I wouldn't mind," Al said dreamily. "We could just kind of float around and look at nature."

"Nature?" I demanded. "How can you think about nature when we're trapped here in the rapids?"

"I've seen bigger rapids in my bathtub," Katie joked.

"Maybe we should send up the flare," Sabs suggested helpfully.

"Patience, Sabs," I said. "We'll have plenty of chances to embarrass ourselves later."

"No problem, you guys," M said calmly. "Remember, when you're in a canoe, you want to get in sync with the river. You want to use the natural energy and harmony out here," M coached us as we drifted along.

"Now, what we need to do is enter the current at an angle," M said. "You know, kind of go with the flow." She paused for a moment and rubbed her forehead in concentration. "Let's try turning the canoe a little to the right, so we'll be aimed in the same direction as the current."

"Easy for you to say," I mumbled.

"It *is* easy, Ran," M replied. "Everybody put your paddles on the left side of the canoe, and stroke."

We all stuck our paddles in and stroked the

way M had suggested. Amazingly enough, it actually worked. The canoe went forward, but veered a little to the right at the same time. We sliced easily into the fast-moving water.

Once the current grabbed us, it was like we were on a train or something. Even without paddling, we were moving right along.

"This is great," I said. "We don't even have to do anything! We can just sit here."

"No, you *must* paddle," M said. "Please keep paddling, girls."

"But why? We're moving, aren't we?"

"Yes, but you're not moving faster than the water."

I shrugged. "Hey, the water's moving plenty fast for me."

But even as I was talking, I noticed that the canoe had begun to drift slightly. We weren't heading forward down the stream anymore. We were heading . . . well, sideways.

"See?" M asked. "If you don't keep the boat moving faster than the water is moving, you can't steer."

We started paddling again, and soon we were pointed downstream. We were even moving faster than the water. But we weren't exactly doing a great job. For one thing, my paddle kept hitting Sabs's paddle. She was taking these fast, little strokes, while I took slower, longer strokes. *Better* strokes, if you ask me.

"How is my hair? Is it frizzing up, you guys?" Sabs asked, pausing to feel her curls. "I hate it when I'm around water. My hair goes completely insane."

"Stop worrying about your hair and watch where you're paddling," I grumbled.

"*Me?*" Sabs asked in a shocked voice. "You're the one who keeps smacking my paddle."

"I can't even see your paddle, because you're behind me. So it's your responsibility to look out for *my* paddle."

"Who made that rule?"

"It's obvious," I said as once again Sabs's paddle knocked against mine.

"Fine," Sabs said. "Let's trade places, and you'll see it isn't exactly easy."

"Fine." I got up carefully, laying my paddle down in the canoe. Sabs climbed to her feet, too, and the boat rocked a little.

"Hey, girls! Rule number one, no standing up in the canoe!" M shouted.

"No prob, M," I said as I gripped Sabs's shoulders and scooted around her. "What do you think I'm going to do? Fall in the water?"

I laughed. Just then my foot caught on a piece of rope that was curled at the bottom of the boat. I clutched at Sabs, but she was falling, too.

The boat rocked wildly, and I threw up both my arms, waving them in the air like a lunatic, trying to catch my balance.

Then, like I was trapped in a movie in slow motion, I felt myself falling backward.

Icy water slapped the back of my neck, and then I was completely submerged, looking up at the bubbles created by my fall. I clawed at the water with my hands and kicked my feet frantically, and all of a sudden I bobbed to the surface like a cork.

As I blinked and sputtered, Sabs popped up next to me. "Boy, these life jackets really work, don't they?" she asked, brushing a dripping tangle of hair from her eyes.

"Girls!" M called anxiously. "Answer me! Are you okay?"

Her question was interrupted by loud laughter. "I'll remember this when *you* fall in," I muttered, twisting around while I treaded water so I could see the smirks on Al's and Katie's faces.

But they weren't the ones laughing. As a matter of fact, they were both looking a little green. And it wasn't because they were seasick. Katie looked at me, then pointed toward shore.

But even before I saw them, I knew who was laughing. There, rolling on the ground in hysterics, were Sam, Greg, Jason, and Nick.

"Excuse me while I drown myself," Sabs moaned.

"Those jerks!" I cried. "I can't believe they've been spying on us this whole time! How did they even know we were here?"

"I guess Sam must have listened in on the extension when we made our plans last night," Sabs said as she treaded water beside me.

Before I could answer her, I heard Greg Loggins shouting at us. "Hey, Zak! I'd give that dive a three-point-one!"

"Nice form," Sam added, "but a little too much splash on the finish."

I took a stroke toward the riverbank, but Sabs grabbed my life jacket. "Where exactly are you going?" she asked.

"Shore," I growled. "I'm going to wring your brother's neck. How would you like me to dispose of the body?"

"Come on, Ran," M said, reaching out her arm. "Climb aboard. There's nothing you can do about those guys right now."

"Wrong, M," I said with fresh determination. "I know exactly what we can do — we can win this race!"

Chapter Five

"Randy, would you mind carrying my books?" Sabs asked on Monday morning as we stood by our lockers. "My arms are killing me."

"Sorry, Sabs," I moaned. "I can't move a muscle, either. It took all my strength just to brush my teeth this morning!"

Sabs leaned against her locker, rubbing her shoulders. "I think maybe we overdid it on Saturday," she said. "We paddled nearly all day."

"Look on the bright side," Al said. "By the end of the day, we actually figured out how to get the canoe to go in a straight line."

"Too bad Sam and the others weren't there to see us," Katie said.

"He's never going to let me forget how I fell in," Sabs said. "You should have heard him yesterday —"

"Never mind," I whispered. "I think we're about to hear for ourselves."

I nodded toward the end of the hall. Sam, Nick, Jason, and Greg were marching toward us, big goofy grins pasted on their faces.

"Well, if it isn't the Klutzoid Canoeing *and* Diving Team," Sam said.

"I'm warning you, Sam," Sabs began angrily, shaking a finger at her brother.

"Maybe we should just call this whole thing off," Nick said loudly — so loudly, in fact, that a few kids stopped to listen. "There's no point in humiliating you frail little girls publicly."

"Hey, watch it!" Greg said gallantly, stepping forward. "You're talking to the weaker sex here."

"Why don't you guys just wait until the real race before you start swaggering?" Al suggested with a very sweet, very fake smile.

"Don't you get it?" Sam said. "We're offering you an easy out here, girls. You can just admit you got carried away and the whole thing will be forgotten."

"Maybe that's not such a bad idea," Sabs whispered, staring at the blisters on her palms.

"Dream on, guys," I said.

"You're the one who's dreaming if you still think you can go up against us," Nick crowed.

"No way are we giving up." I said it quickly, without looking at any of my friends, but out of the corner of my eye, I noticed Sabs rolling her eyes. "As a matter of fact," I continued, "I think we ought to raise the stakes a little —"

"No more bets!" Sabs and Katie both cried at exactly the same moment.

"Name it!" Sam said with a grin. "The bigger the stakes, the better!"

I tapped my finger on my chin. "I'm thinking of something more important than chores, or even money . . . I'm thinking we should put your egos on the line, guys."

Nick frowned. "Our egos?"

"You know. Those huge, overinflated bags of hot air you're carrying around with you?"

Just then I noticed some guy walking down the hall with a T-shirt that had BRADLEY WILD CATS, the name of our school baseball team, written on the front. Suddenly it came to me.

"I've got it! The losers will have to agree to wear something truly humiliating for an entire day here at school, where everyone can see it. T-shirts printed with something."

"I don't know, Randy," Al murmured doubtfully.

"Don't worry," I assured her. "We're not the ones who are going to have to wear them!"

"But what should they say?" Sam asked.

"How about 'Jock Wannabe'?" Nick suggested.

"Or 'Member of the Weaker Sex'?" Greg added.

"I know!" I said. "'Sports Wimp.' It's short and sweet and says it all."

"Perfect!" Sam agreed. "You're on, Zak! I think you're out of your mind, but you're on!"

"By the way," Sabs muttered, "I wear an Extra Small."

Okay. Maybe I should have kept my mouth shut about the T-shirts. But it was just a harmless little bet, I figured.

What I didn't figure on was the fact that pretty soon the whole school would be wagering on the Great Canoe Race. And I do mean the *whole* school.

"This is really getting out of hand," I complained during lunch on Thursday. "This morning in Italian class, Sonya and Kelly made a bet with Josh and Tyrone on the race. If we win, Josh and Tyrone have to come to school the next day wearing white gym socks, dress shoes, and shorts."

"What if we lose?" Al asked as she opened her milk carton.

I sighed. "Then Sonya and Kelly have to wear their clothes inside out for an entire day."

"Too bad for them. Why didn't you warn them we don't have a prayer?" Sabs asked.

"I did, but they said something about us being united in sisterhood," I replied, reaching across the table to steal one of Sabs's potato chips. "I don't mind making my own bets, but I can't stand having this much responsibility for other people's. The entire female population of the school is counting on us."

"Like Jenna Walker," Katie said. "I ran into her in the girls' room this morning. She'd just bet Mike that if we won, he'd have to walk backward in the halls for an entire day! If the guys won, she'd have to do it." Katie sighed. "She asked me what I thought our chances were."

"What did you tell her?" Sabs asked.

"I told her that if she started practicing now, she'd probably have walking backward down to a science by the time we lost."

I unwrapped my sandwich and stared at it long and hard.

"Are you sure that's edible?" Sabs demanded, wrinkling her nose at my lunch.

"Not exactly," I admitted. "I overslept this morning, so I just slapped together whatever I could find lying around in the fridge. I found this in a bag of stuff M bought at The Good Earth — you know, that health food store on Main Street?" I sniffed at the pasty white- and-green goop oozing out of a piece of pita bread. "I think it's a pretty safe guess that tofu's some-how involved."

"Here." Al passed me half of her peanut butter and jelly sandwich.

"Thanks," I said gratefully. "I owe you."

"You may owe a lot of people before this race is over," Al warned. "You haven't made any more bets, have you?"

"Well . . . " I paused, suddenly *very* interested in the peanut butter and jelly sandwich.

"Randy!" Al exclaimed. "You promised!"

"This doesn't involve the rest of us, I hope," Katie said, frowning at me as she peeled a banana.

"You'll thank me for making these bets," I said quickly.

"*These?*" Al cried. "You mean, there's more than one?"

"I couldn't help myself," I admitted. "Yesterday in the hall Nick and Jason were going on and on about how they were going to cream us. I told them they were getting overconfident —"

"They have a *right* to be overconfident," Al reminded me.

"And anyway," I continued, "we sort of sweetened the pot a little."

"Sweetened the pot?" Sabs repeated.

"Sabs, one of these days I'm going to have to teach you to play poker," I said with a laugh. "We just added a couple of new elements to the bet."

"Such as?" Katie asked, her arms crossed over her chest.

"Well, for starters, the losers have to bow to the winners every time they see them —"

"Oh, no!" Sabs moaned. "No way am I bowing to Sam all day long! His ego's already going to be the size of the Goodyear Blimp!"

"And," I added under my breath, "losers have to serve winners lunch at school." I paused, waiting for the groans, but my friends were just staring at me with stunned expressions.

"Homemade lunch," I added in a near-whisper. "Including dessert."

Sabs was the first to speak. "Isn't it enough that you dragged us into this thing?" she cried. "Talk about adding insult to injury!"

"I-I'm sorry, guys. It just sort of popped out. They were being so cocky and obnoxious, I *had* to say something, didn't I?"

"*No!*" all three shouted in unison, so loudly that people turned to stare.

"All right, already," I said. "This time I really promise — no more bets, no matter what."

"Big deal," Katie said. "You've run out of people to bet with, anyway."

"I have an idea," Al said suddenly. "Let's go to the principal and complain about all the gambling taking place on school property. Maybe he could make some kind of announcement, canceling all the bets —"

"Are you kidding?" Sabs interrupted, rolling her eyes. "I heard that Mr. Hansen has a bet going with Ms. Underwood on the race!"

"The principal and the vice principal!" I cried. "What's the bet?"

"Something to do with supervising detentions for a week," Sabs replied.

"I take it Mr. Hansen doesn't think we have a shot at winning?" I asked.

"Neither does Stacy," Katie said. Stacy is the principal's daughter, the self-appointed queen of Bradley. You might say she and I aren't exactly good friends. As a matter of fact, you might just say that we can't stand each other.

"Stacy and the clones are the only girls I know who are betting on the guys to win," Sabs said as she munched on a carrot stick. The clones are Stacy's friends B. Z. Latimer, Eva Malone, and Laurel Spencer, who follow Stacy around like lost puppies.

"You mean, they're actually betting against us?" I demanded. "How could they be such traitors to their own sex?"

"Of course we're betting against you."

I twisted in my seat to see Stacy approaching, with Eva, B.Z., and Laurel on her heels.

"We heard about your first practice, Rowena," Stacy said in a sugary-sweet voice. Rowena is my real name, but Stacy is the only one who actually uses it. She just does it to get under my skin. Unfortunately, it works like a charm.

"Thank goodness you didn't *drown*," Stacy added. "I didn't realize leather floated."

Stacy and I have this ongoing argument about fashion. She thinks I have lousy taste. I don't think she has any taste at all. Today, for example, Stacy was dressed in a pale peach–and–white jumpsuit. She looked like a Creamsicle with an attitude.

"Speaking of drowning," I said, just as sweetly, "maybe you'd like to come along on our next canoe ride, Stace?"

"I think I'll pass," Stacy replied.

"I don't suppose you could pass up a good bet, though, could you?" I asked.

Al shot me a warning look that could have melted glass, but I had other things on my mind.

"Bet?" Stacy asked warily. "What kind of bet?"

"Let's see," I said, tapping my fingernails on the table.

"Leave us out of this one!" Sabs hissed.

"Hmm," I murmured, running through various options. The idea of publicly humiliating Stacy was quite inspiring. "Suppose we make this a bet with a fashion payoff?"

"Randy," Katie whispered, *just say no!*

"I like the sound of this," Stacy said with a

sneer. "What exactly did you have in mind?"

"If we win, you agree to dress in black leather clothes for an entire week."

Stacy swallowed hard. She does not consider black a color, let alone a color she might actually wear.

"Why not?" Eva whispered to Stacy. "It's not like they have a prayer of winning!"

"Good point," Stacy said with a tilt of her chin. "Fine, Rowena. The bet's on. But if you lose, you've got to agree to wear nothing but pastels for a week" — she paused, considering — "with a matching bow in your hair!"

"Randy," Al said in a low voice, "you don't even *own* anything pastel!"

"So?" I said. I threw back my shoulders and gave Stacy my best "What, me worry?" stare. "You're on, Stace." I extended my hand, and after a moment's hesitation, Stacy shook it gingerly. She was wearing peach polish, with little white flowers painted on her long nails. Suddenly I lost my appetite.

"You'll be sorry, *Stace*," I added as she strutted off.

"Correction," Sabs said when she was safely out of earshot. "*You'll* be sorry, *Rowena*."

"I've got some pastel bows you can borrow," Katie volunteered.

"I won't be needing them," I said confidently. Then I paused, looked around at my friends, and dropped my head to the table with a sigh. "Do you have some clothes I could borrow, too?" I muttered.

Chapter Six

The next day, which was Friday, Al, Katie, Sabs, and I were heading toward my house after school when I heard someone call my name.

I turned and saw Greg and Sam waving at us. "Hey, Randy!" Greg called again.

I turned back, ignoring him, hoping it looked like I was too busy talking to my friends to bother answering.

Just my luck. Greg wasn't the kind of guy to take a hint.

"Hey, Randy!" he yelled. "Going swimming again tomorrow?"

"Why don't you guys get a life?" I yelled back, spinning around.

"We don't want to miss your next practice," Sam yelled, obviously not intimidated by my scowl. "We were thinking about going to see that new movie that everyone says is so funny, but then we realized, hey, what could possibly be funnier than watching the four of you try to paddle a canoe?"

"I'm going to see if I can borrow my dad's videocamera," Greg added. "I'd love to catch your act on tape so I can watch again and again."

"Very funny," I muttered. Not much of a comeback, I know, but there wasn't much else I could say. It wasn't like I could deny that our practice had been pathetic. We were well on our way to being the laughingstocks of Bradley Junior High.

"Just ignore them," Sabs advised. "I've been ignoring Sam all my life."

"I can't face going back to the river tomorrow and looking like a dweeb again," Katie said.

Suddenly an idea hit me. "Why *should* we go back there tomorrow?"

"Because it's too late to back out," Katie answered, "and if we don't practice at all, we'll not only lose, we'll stink."

"I didn't mean that we shouldn't practice," I explained. "But why should we do it on Saturday, when the guys will be waiting to spy on us?"

"Good point," Al said, nodding thoughtfully. "When could we go instead?"

I shrugged. "Why not right now? Let's ask
M if she can take us."

"Randy's right," Katie agreed. "If we have
to look like total dweebs, at least let's do it in
private!"

When we got to my house, we found M in
her studio. Luckily, she was done working for
the day, so I didn't mind asking if she could
take us to the river.

"Sure, I'll take you," she agreed as she finished cleaning up her work space. "It's nice to
see the way you girls are really starting to enjoy
this."

We all looked at each other. I'm not sure
who started laughing first, but once we started,
it was awfully hard to stop.

"Was it something I said?" M demanded as
we headed out the door, shaking our heads.

We piled into the car and drove down to the
river. As usual, Brendan was working at the
canoe-rental counter.

"Back again?" he asked.

"We believe that suffering builds character,"

I explained.

"Hey, I talked to Mr. Loggins, Greg's dad, about the race your kids are having," Brendan said to M. "He suggested a two-part race. The first leg would be to the picnic area, which is about one hour downstream. Then there would be a one-hour lunch-and-rest period. I would be there to check the times of the teams, and whichever team gets to the picnic area first gets to leave first."

"You mean, when my girls get to the picnic area five minutes ahead of the boys, they get to leave five minutes ahead of the boys after lunch?" M asked.

Brendan nodded. "Yeah, then it's about another hour to the finish line."

M looked over at me. "Does that sound okay?"

I shrugged. "Whatever."

Brendan got our canoe ready, and we all climbed in, including M. Fortunately, by this point we at least realized how to get the canoe away from the shore. Major progress.

Amazingly enough, we seemed to have remembered a few other things from our first, disastrous practice. Like not standing up in the boat.

"So far, so good," Al joked. "We've gone a hundred yards and no one's fallen in yet."

"Let's try and see if we can coordinate our strokes a little better this time," M suggested.

"Yeah, we need to try and work together as a team," Katie said enthusiastically.

I rolled my eyes, but I had to admit that Katie was right. We *were* supposed to be a team, after all.

"At Camp Winotonka my canoe team would sing a song as we paddled," M said wistfully.

"No way, M," I shot back. "I'm not singing any nerdy camp song out here."

"The song doesn't matter, Randy," M said. "It's the rhythm. Keeping a beat helps everyone know when to paddle. The way you keep a beat for Iron Wombat," M added, referring to the rock band I play drums for.

"Now, if we could only fit my drum set in this canoe, we'd get our act together out here," I said.

"How about improvising?" M suggested. "One of you can call out a rhythm."

"Randy should do it," Katie said. "She's the drummer, after all."

"I agree," Sabs said. "Besides, this whole thing was her dumb idea to begin with."

"Okay, okay. I'll do it," I said. I wasn't sure M's keeping-the-beat idea was going to help. But it was better than singing some dumb camp song. Besides, Sabs's last remark made me feel pretty guilty. "How about if I call out 'Stroke'? When I say that, your paddles should all hit the water at the same time."

"At the beginning or at the end?" Sabs asked.

"What?"

"Should the paddle hit the water as you *start* to say 'Stroke,' or should we wait until you're done saying it?"

Good question. I had no idea, since I'd never been the rhythm section for a canoe team before. "Okay," I said after a moment, "when I say 'Str——,' you bring your paddle down, and by the time I say ' ——oke,' your paddle should hit the water."

"Then when does it come back up?" Al asked.

"Just make sure you're ready for the next time she says 'Stroke,'" M interjected, "and I'm sure everything will work out fine."

"Okay, everyone ready?" I said. "*S-s-troke!*"

To my amazement it actually seemed to work. None of the paddles tangled, and the canoe shot forward. "Stroke!" I yelled again, and sure enough, the canoe moved even faster.

"Hey, it's working," Al marveled.

"Of course it's working," M said happily. "I mean, it's not like this is quantum physics."

"Or brain surgery," Sabs said.

"Or rocket science," Katie said.

"Or nuclear chemistry," Al said.

"Stroke!" I called.

We were actually moving down the stream in a nice straight line, faster than we had ever gone before.

"You know, Sam is going to be so disappointed when he sees our next practice and we're paddling so well," Sabs said happily.

"You're right," I said. "Stroke! Those guys would be amazed. Stroke!"

"Knowing them, they'd probably try to weasel out of their bets," Al said. "If we keep going like this and practice hard, we could actually almost win."

"The only problem is, once the guys figure out we're getting better, they're going to start practicing more," Katie said, leaning into each stroke of her paddle.

"Yeah, now they're overconfident," I said. "Stroke! But if they realize . . . Stroke! Wait a minute! I just . . . Stroke! I just had an idea!"

Sabs glanced over her shoulder at me. "Are you thinking what I think you're thinking?"

"I think so," I said.

Katie turned around and grinned. "I think I know what Sabs thinks you're thinking," she said. "Why should we let them know we're getting better? Why not let them *stay* overconfident?"

"Exactly!" I cried. "Stroke! We practice tomorrow . . . Stroke! Only, we deliberately look pathetic . . . Stroke! And the guys will think they've . . . Stroke! . . . got it made."

"Now we're starting to use our heads!" Al exclaimed. "And if we use our brains as well as our muscles, we really just might beat those guys."

Since Sam had been finding out about our practice sessions by eavesdropping on Sabrina, on Friday night, just to make sure that the boys would know where to find us, I called the Wells house for a "fake" phone call with Sabs.

Sure enough, about two seconds after Sabs came on the line, we heard a telltale click as Sam picked up the extension. Then Sabs and I "confirmed" the team's practice plans for Saturday. When I hung up, I was laughing so hard, I could barely dial Al's number to report that phase one of our plan had worked like a charm.

On Saturday morning we were totally psyched. We got to the river at our usual time and piled into the canoe-rental shop to get our equipment. M decided we could handle our little scheme by ourselves. While she stayed on-shore and talked to Brendan, the four of us paddled out into the river.

We moved along smoothly until we neared the place where the boys had spied on us the previous Saturday.

"Do you see them?" Sabs whispered.

Allison shook her head. "How can we be so sure they're going to show up today?"

"Right after Randy called me, I heard Sam call Greg and make plans to come here again," Sabs said smugly. "*Two* can play at the tele-phone-extension game."

"Shh!" Allison subtly nodded toward a stand of trees on an overhang above the river. "It's them! And I think Greg has a videocamera."

"Excellent!" I said. "Everyone ready?"

"Ready," Sabs said, nodding.

"Ready," Katie said through gritted teeth.

"I'm ready, too," Allison said.

"All right, then, Operation Deception begins . . . now!" I deliberately reached up and tangled my paddle with Sabs's. "Hey, watch what you're doing!" I yelled at her at the top of my lungs.

"Me? You're the clumsy one!" Sabs shouted back, using her paddle to push mine away. Meanwhile, the canoe was drifting sideways in the current.

"Stop fighting, you two!" Allison scolded while Sabs and I continued our paddle duel.

"Paddles on the right!" Katie yelled, and we all stopped fighting and stuck our paddles into the water on the right side of the canoe. Naturally, we tangled together and sent the boat spinning.

"Harder!" Katie cried, sounding half-hysterical.

We began paddling faster than ever, our paddles slamming against each other as we stroked at totally different speeds. We were spinning furiously now, going round and round as the current carried us along.

"Paddles left!" I shouted, and we all switched sides at once and began paddling just as insanely in the other direction. Soon we were doing a nice reverse spin.

I glanced up toward the overhang. Greg was laughing so hard, he could barely hang on to his videocamera. Sam and Jason were rolling on the ground, holding their sides. And I couldn't be positive, but it sure looked like Nick was laughing so hard, he was crying.

"Change places!" Sabs shouted suddenly. And just as we had rehearsed, we all jumped up at once and tried to switch seats. For about a minute the canoe rocked crazily back and forth while we played musical chairs. Then, when the time was right, Allison let herself fall back into the water with a splash.

I heard an explosion of laughter from the guys.

"Save her!" I yelled to Katie, trying to sound panicky. Katie immediately dived in. Both she and Al were swept away downstream, screaming and yelling all the way.

"I'll save you!" I shouted, diving in next and leaving Sabs alone in the canoe.

"Wait!" Sabs wailed. "You can't leave me here all alone!" And with that, she jumped in with a tremendous splash.

As we were carried off downstream, our canoe twisted and spun nearby, following us along on the current. I caught a last glimpse of the guys, still laughing hysterically, as we were whisked around a sharp bend.

"Perfect," I said under my breath. "Enjoy your laugh while you can, macho men."

As soon as we were out of sight, Katie reached under the water and began pulling on the rope that was tied around her ankle and attached to the canoe. In a few seconds she managed to pull it to her. The rest of us joined up with her, holding the canoe still while she climbed in.

"They bought it," I said as I slithered over the side and got back to my seat. "They totally fell for it!"

"I could hear Sam laughing the whole time," Sabs said with a satisfied sigh.

Katie gave me a high-five. "Good plan, Randy!"

I grinned. "Ready, girls?" I asked, picking up my paddle.

"Ready!" they agreed.

"Then . . . Stroke!"

Chapter Seven

"Where's everyone going?" I asked when I entered the school lobby on Monday morning.

People usually move in slow motion on Monday, like they're slowly figuring out that the weekend's over. But today, for some reason, kids were rushing down the hall like they were on their way to pick up free concert tickets.

Allison shook her head. "I have no idea."

"Hey, Arizonna, what's going on?" I called when I saw him cruise past.

He shrugged. "I don't exactly know, babe, only someone said Greg and Sam have this really funny video they made. They're down in the audiovisual lab, showing it now." Before I could ask anything more, he dashed off with the rest of the crowd.

"A really funny video," I repeated under my breath. "You don't think —"

Al grinned. "I'll bet you it is."

"No more bets!" I exclaimed. I grabbed Al's arm and we merged into the stream of people heading down the hall toward the AV lab. "Let's check it out."

A huge crowd of students was jammed into the tiny room. As I had suspected, Greg and Sam were standing on either side of a TV set, working a VCR with the remote control. Al and I found a place near the back of the crowd.

"Show it again!" someone yelled.

"Gladly, gladly," Sam agreed. "It just gets better each time you see it."

He rewound the tape and then hit the PLAY button. The photography wasn't great, but you could definitely see me, Sabs, Katie, and Al, standing up in our canoe and rocking back and forth crazily until all four of us eventually ended up in the water.

As each of us fell in, the crowd broke up. When the tape was over, they applauded and cheered, begging Sam to run it again. This time he ran it backward at high speed so it looked like we were leaping out of the water and into the boat.

"This is better than the Three Stooges!" some guy yelled.

"Yeah, it's the Four Stooges!" Sam agreed.

Al and I discreetly backed away before anyone could notice us. "By the end of the day, every person in school will have either seen this tape or heard about it," Al said when we were back in the hall. "We'll be the total laughingstocks of Bradley Junior High."

I nodded. "People will think we're the most pathetic, hopeless canoers on the planet. No one will think we have a chance of winning."

Al and I exchanged grins. "We got'em," she said.

"So far, so good," I agreed.

For the rest of the week, we practiced canoeing every afternoon after school for two solid hours. Sabs eavesdropped on one of Sam's phone calls Monday night and learned that we were safe from the guys' spying on us again. Since Greg had made that stupid video of us, the guys decided they didn't need to go all the way to the river to get a good laugh out of our practice sessions. They could just pop in the video.

By Friday afternoon we were totally pumped and ready to go. We figured we deserved a break from practicing and decided to go over to the mall. I'm not big on mall-crawling, personally, but even *I* was glad to be hanging out on dry land for a change.

"Boy, it's such a relief not to be to paddling a canoe for once," Sabs said, pausing to look over an outfit on a storefront mannequin.

"I can't wait till this canoe race is over," Katie said. "It's not easy for me to play along with being the school dork. If I hear the name Four Stooges or Canoe Clowns one more time, I just might scream."

"I know it's tough," I said as I pulled Sabs away from a display of brightly colored watches. "But you have to admit, it's working beautifully. Whatever humiliation we're putting up with now will be nothing next to what they'll have to deal with when we win."

"*If* we win," Al added darkly.

"Confidence, team, confidence." I pointed to a shop across from the food court. "There's the store I was looking for."

"Are you going to let us in on this latest scheme of yours?" Sabs demanded.

"Sure. We're going into that T-shirt store to buy four large 'University of Minnesota' sweatshirts."

"We are?" Katie asked doubtfully.

"But I don't need a sweatshirt," Sabs argued. "Although, now that you mention it, I could use a pair of shorts —"

"Listen up," I interrupted. "So far, what have we done? We've gotten really good at handling our canoe, *and* we've made the guys think we're really bad, right?"

Everyone nodded.

"But what happens on the day of the race when we jump in our canoe and take off at high speed?"

"We win?" Sabs guessed.

"Maybe so, and then again, maybe not," I said. "We have to be realistic. No matter how hard we've trained, those guys still have more upper-body strength. You know — longer arms, bigger shoulders. Chances are, they can still paddle harder and faster than us, especially since we haven't been working out for very long. And as soon as they see that we're zooming along, they're really going to pour on the speed."

"If the guys are going to win anyway, how come we've been training so hard?" Sabs asked.

I grinned. "Because now we're so good that

we just need one more little thing before we *can* win. And that one little thing is this," I said, tapping the side of my head.

"Hair?" Sabs asked, frowning.

"No, brains," I said. "See, it's really very simple. If the guys see us racing along, they'll do everything they can to beat us. But if they think we're still way back behind them —"

Katie grinned. "Then they'll take it easy," she said. "As long as they're sure we're far behind them, they won't even bother to paddle fast."

"But how do we convince them we're way behind when we hope we're going to be way out in front?" Al demanded.

I wiggled my eyebrows in a conspiratorial way. "We go in and buy four maroon-and-gold 'University of Minnesota' sweatshirts, that's how."

"I still don't get this," Sabs said, shaking her head.

"You will," I assured her. "And so will the guys — but they'll get it too late!"

When we were done at the mall, we all returned to my house. We had decided it would be easier if everybody slept over. That way we'd have plenty of time the next morning to get psyched for the race.

We were pretty much starving by the time we got home, so I started rummaging around the fridge to see what I could dig up. "Good news, guys!" I reported. "There's a whole gallon of pralines-and-cream ice cream in the freezer!"

"Ice cream! Are you crazy?" M cried, marching into the kitchen with this shocked look on her face. "You can't eat ice cream for dinner!"

"I meant for dessert, M," I replied. Which wasn't entirely true, I have to admit.

M shook her head firmly. "No way. All that fat and sugar? What you need to do is load up on complex carbohydrates tonight and tomorrow morning. They're a good, solid source of energy."

"What exactly do you mean when you say carbohydrates?" I asked suspiciously.

"Things like bread, potatoes, and pasta. That's why I made a huge batch of pasta for you."

"*You* cooked?" I asked, trying not to sound too doubtful. Around my house we eat a lot of take-out Chinese food and pizza.

"Don't look at me like I'm trying to poison you!" M said with a laugh. "I'm still your coach, aren't I? So, since I know you girls need to carb up tonight, I bought fresh pasta at the market and some prepared marinara sauce."

"Pasta marinara?" I said. "That sounds good."

"What's pasta marinara?" Al asked.

"It's spaghetti with tomato sauce," Katie explained.

Sabs rolled her eyes. "You New Yorkers! Can't you just say spaghetti when you mean spaghetti?"

Half an hour later, under M's watchful eye, we gorged on pasta — spaghetti, that is — until we were stuffed. Until we were *way* past stuffed.

"You're not going to make us eat more of this in the morning, are you?" I asked, pushing my chair away from the table.

"No, but you will have to eat plenty of cereal and muffins. Also, I want you to drink lots of juices and water. You'll see — you'll have all kinds of energy."

"I hope so," I said. "We'll need it."

We watched a little TV with M, then headed

up to my room. I got into bed, and everyone else crawled into their sleeping bags.

We had planned to go right to sleep, since we figured we could use a good, long night's rest. But it was hard to fall asleep right away.

"Do you think we can really win?" Sabs asked softly as we all lay there in the dark.

"We can win. And we *will* win," I said, sounding more confident than I felt.

"Randy's plan will work," Al said.

"Besides, we're in great shape," Katie pointed out. "And we've practiced hard."

"You're right," Sabs said contentedly. "Plus, don't forget all that spaghetti we ate! We'll kick their butts."

We all fell silent for a moment. "Still . . ." Katie said quietly, "maybe we should try a little something extra."

"Like what?" I asked. It seemed to me we'd thought of everything.

"Well, I don't know exactly," Katie replied. "Maybe we could rub Vaseline all over the handles of their paddles, or something!"

We all laughed. "Or we could spray itching powder on their life jackets," Al suggested. "It would drive them nuts."

"We won't need to cheat to beat those guys," I said, yawning. "We'll beat them fair and square."

"You're absolutely right," Sabs agreed.

"We should get to sleep," I said. "We do have a big day ahead of us."

The last thing I heard before I drifted off to sleep was Sabs saying, "Of course, we could put Krazy Glue on the seats of their canoe. . . ."

It seemed like just a few seconds later when I sat bolt upright in my bed. The room was bright with sunshine.

"*What* is that noise?" I moaned.

Incredibly loud music was blaring through the house. The walls of my room seemed to be vibrating with each new trumpet blast. It sounded like an entire marching band was stomping toward my bedroom.

"I'm awake already!" Katie yelled. She leaped out of her sleeping bag, then looked around in confusion.

"Sam, turn that down!" Sabs moaned, pulling her pillow over her head.

Suddenly the door of my room flew open, and I saw M, completely dressed in her canoe-coaching outfit — sneakers, khaki shorts, and a T-shirt that said, A WOMAN'S PLACE IS IN THE HOUSE — AND THE SENATE. She also had on a baseball cap, and sunglasses dangling from a cord around her neck. I was relieved that she had stopped short of wearing a whistle. With the door open, the music sounded even louder. But M just shouted over it.

"Time to rise and shine, team!" she cried.

"Five more minutes, M — please?" I begged.

"Sorry, Ran. It's time to get moving," M insisted. "Let the games begin!" she said as she stepped over to my bed and yanked the covers off.

"Thanks, Coach," I said with a groan. Having no other choice, I climbed out of my bed. "Hey, you guys, let's go," I said, trying my best to sound awake. "Let's go, team!"

Unfortunately, M's peppy wake-up call had not quite inspired the team. Sabs still had a pillow over her head, Katie was groaning something about "just one more hour," and Al was sinking back into the depths of her sleeping bag. Only the very top of her head was visible.

"You have carbohydrates to load up on, kids," M reminded them.

"Wait a second," I said, winking at M. "I know what will work." I took a deep breath. "Stroke!" I shouted.

Instantly, like the well-oiled paddling machine they were, Sabs, Katie, and Al threw their pillows at me.

Chapter Eight

"I have never seen this many people down at the river before," Brendan said when we got there. "There must be a thousand people here."

He was exaggerating just a little, but it was true that both banks of the river were covered with people. It was mostly kids, but there were plenty of adults, too.

A lot of them had banners and signs, the boys especially. They were carrying signs that said things like BOYS ARE JUST BETTER and GIVE UP, CANOE CLOWNS. I saw Stacy and her clones carrying a big sign that said GIRLS FOR THE BOYS' TEAM.

Stacy and her group were the only traitors. All of the other girls were backing our team, although I don't think any of them expected us to win. But it was nice to see a few signs supporting our team: GIRLS CAN DO IT!, BOYS ARE BOGUS, and BRADLEY BABES ARE NUMBER ONE!

It was like a beach party. People had brought food, blankets, and fold-up chairs. There were at least three portable stereos playing three different tapes — one rap, one rock, and one reggae — which just combined to make the whole situation even louder and more confusing than it already was.

"I wish all these people weren't here," Sabs said anxiously as we pulled our stuff out of the trunk of M's car.

"Why?" Katie asked.

"You know how frizzy my hair gets when it's wet. I really don't need all these people looking at me and going, 'Wow, look at her hair. She really should do something about that frizz.'" She pulled a huge knapsack out of the trunk and sighed.

"What's that?" I asked.

"This?" Sabs echoed innocently. "Just a few things I thought I might need during the race."

"Like what?"

"Like . . . my sweatshirt," she paused, "and a hairbrush."

I gazed at her skeptically. "That looks like more than a sweatshirt and a hairbrush."

In fact, it was so big, Sabs was having trouble keeping up with us as she clutched it to her chest with both arms. I guess she was afraid that she might tip over if she put it on her back.

"Well, maybe there's a comb and some hair spray. And some hair mousse, just in case things get totally out of control. Plus a little makeup so I'll look good crossing the finish line."

"Sabs! We have to paddle all that extra weight," I protested.

"It's not very heavy. Besides, I *am* the smallest person on the team, you know. I weigh less than any of you three, so I figured I was entitled to some extra weight."

I had to laugh. Sabs has a special kind of logic that only she understands. But the truth was, a few pounds more or less wasn't going to make much difference. If we beat the guys, we would beat them by a lot. It probably wasn't going to be a close call.

"I don't mind the extra weight as long as you let me use some of that stuff, too," Katie said. "Here, I'll even carry it for you," she added obligingly. She took the knapsack from Sabs and slipped it on her shoulders.

We headed down to the water, lugging our

pack of food, the duffel bag where we kept our secret weapons, and, of course, Sabs's portable beauty shop.

The Big Bad Boys, as the boys' team had nicknamed themselves, were already down by the water where the two canoes were beached side by side. Sam and his friends were hanging out with a bunch of other guys and looked totally cool about the race.

"Hey, it's the losers," Greg shouted gleefully as we strode toward them.

"It's the Canoe Clowns," Sam yelled. "The Four Stooges!"

"Hey, nice life jackets," Jason said. "Some snorkels and fins would come in handy, too. Don't you think?"

"Yeah, well, " I said sheepishly, hanging my head. "I guess we do fall in sometimes."

"Anyone can fall in the water," Katie said defensively. "In fact, I don't know if you noticed, but there was a team of guys from the University of Minnesota paddling around out here a little while ago, and one of them looked wet."

"A team from the University of Minnesota?" Sam asked curiously. "How do you know that's where they were from?"

"Well," I said, feeling pleased at how easily the guys were taking our bait, "they were all wearing maroon-and-gold sweatshirts that said 'University of Minnesota' on them. They said we'd probably run into them later on. They're going to be on the river practicing all day."

Sam snorted derisively. "Knowing you girls, you probably *will* run into them — literally!"

"Yeah, I hope they don't laugh so hard, they tip over," Greg added. Sam and he exchanged high-fives.

"Well, anyway, if you see four guys in U of M sweatshirts, at least you'll know who they are," Katie said, smiling.

"We'll tell them you said hi," Greg replied, rolling his eyes.

Just then Brendan walked over. "Time to get this show on the road," he said, clapping his hands briskly.

"Good luck, girls," Greg said snidely, coming by to give us one last hard time. Katie spun around, looking very much like she wanted to belt him. She turned, and the knapsack slipped and fell to the ground.

As Katie quickly bent down to pick it up, I

noticed that a maroon sweatshirt sleeve with a gold stripe was sticking out of the pack.

"Allow me," Greg said, trying to help as she slipped her arms through the straps and settled it on her back. Fortunately, he didn't seem to notice the sweatshirt. Katie's squirming, as she tried to escape Greg's help, was probably a good distraction. Once the pack was in place, he gave a mocking bow and headed for his own canoe.

"Time to get ready," Brendan said amiably as he checked to make sure each person was wearing a life jacket.

"Okay, team," M said. "Just remember all you've learned, and everything will be fine."

"We're cool, M," I said calmly as we settled into our places. I think she was more fired up even than we were.

"Well, I'll be waiting for you down at the finish line. Along with the rest of this crowd," she added, glancing around at the spectators.

"We'll be there," I said. "Stop worrying. It's only a canoe race. It's not like it's brain surgery."

"Or quantum physics," M said with a smile.

"Or rocket science," Al added, completing the list.

"Okay, teams," Brendan called out. "Everyone

ready? Men's team?"

The guys responded with a chorus of grunts.

"All ready on the women's team?" Brendan called.

"Ready to go!" I called, trying to sound confident.

"Paddles up!" Brendan shouted.

We all raised our paddles.

"On your marks, get set . . . *go!*"

A roar went up from the crowd as the boys' team sliced the water with their paddles. Their canoe leaped out into the current.

I slammed my paddle back against Sabs's, yelling "Stroke! Stroke! Stroke!" impossibly fast. Our canoe lurched out a few feet and began spinning crazily in the current while the four of us shouted and squealed like idiots.

I could hear the girls onshore groaning, and the boys — along with Stacy and her clones — laughing harder than ever. We must have looked like totally hopeless losers. While the guys moved confidently and smoothly, we just spun in aimless circles.

It was perfect.

We kept up the act until we rounded the bend,

out of sight of the crowd. Up ahead we could see the guys, but they were pulling away fast.

"Let them get a little farther away," I cautioned. "We don't want them to know what we're up to."

"Good start," Allison commented.

"Perfect," I agreed. "I only hope the rest of the plan works as well."

"Well, we'll know by the time we reach the halfway point and stop for lunch."

"I can barely see them now," Al said, shading her eyes to look off into the distance.

"Okay, Operation Deception, part two!" I announced.

As Sabs took her UNIVERSITY OF MINNESOTA sweatshirt out of her knapsack, Al grabbed the duffel bag and began handing them out to the rest of us, as well as stocking caps. We pulled the sweatshirts on right over our life jackets, which made us look like huge-shouldered guys. Then we tucked up all our hair under the stocking caps.

"Ready?" I asked.

"Ready!" the team replied with determined voices.

"Then . . . Stroke!"

Our paddles sliced the water in perfect unison, and the canoe shot forward. We found the fastest part of the current and really started moving. It took a while, but soon the boys' canoe was back in view.

"We're gaining on them!" Katie said excitedly.

I called out the strokes in a low voice, and we quickly moved up on the guys. Even from a distance we could tell that they were horsing around as much as they were paddling. They kept hugging the shoreline, checking out girls who were sunbathing on the banks of the river.

"Excellent!" Al said. "They're acting just as overconfident as we'd hoped."

"It's *better* than we'd hoped," I said. "Stroke!"

Then, to our amazement, the guys actually stopped paddling. Greg called out to some girl on the shore. I could hear him telling her where he went to school.

In a flash we passed them. "They're watching us!" Sabs hissed.

"I know," I said. "But are they following us?"

Sabs glanced over her shoulder again. "No!

I think they fell for it!"

I turned around and saw Greg looking back upstream, like he was waiting to see if we were catching up. Then he looked over at us and actually waved. "Go, Minnesota!" he yelled in a voice we could only faintly hear.

I kept my head down and waved back.

"We did it!" Katie said.

"We haven't won yet," I cautioned.

"Randy's right," Al agreed. "This is no time for *us* to start getting overconfident."

We paddled as hard as we could for the next hour. The guys' team was nowhere to be seen. We had just rounded a bend in the river when we saw the sign that Stacy and her clones had set up at the lunch stop.

"'Welcome, Big Bad Boys!'" Allison read aloud.

"What? No one's here to welcome *us*?" I said, laughing.

We headed the canoe toward shore, feeling tired and very hungry. Sabs was the first to jump ashore, followed by me, then Al and Katie. We pulled the canoe up onto the shore and quickly tied it to a tree branch.

Brendan came strolling up, holding a stopwatch. "Hey, we're using this spot for a race, guys —" he began.

Before he could finish, we pulled off our caps and shook out our hair.

His eyes went wide. Instantly he checked his watch and marked our time down on his clipboard. Then he just looked at us and shook his head, grinning. "Good trick, ladies," he said. "So, how far back are the guys?"

I shrugged. "Who knows? We haven't seen them."

"They are going to be really annoyed," he said, laughing. "But maybe this will teach them a lesson — never underestimate your opponent!"

We walked up the bank to a little campground. Stacy and three of her friends were cooking hot dogs over a charcoal fire. I picked up a plate and snuck up behind Stacy.

"Hey, Stace, let me have a hot dog," I said in a gruff guy's voice, trying to sound like Greg.

She spun around and froze, with her mouth half-open. *"Y-you?"*

"Yes, it's m-me," I said, imitating her stammer. Then I just stood there grinning at her.

It was well worth the whole morning of

paddling just to see the expression on Stacy's face.

Chapter Nine

"What are you doing here?" Stacy demanded, a horrified look on her face. "Where are the
guys?"

"They're . . . well, to be honest, we passed
those Big Bad Boys so long ago that I'm not
really sure where they are." I reached past her
and nimbly lifted a hot dog from the grill onto a
bun.

"Those aren't for you!"

I took a big bite and grinned at her. "Oh,
sorry. Here, you want it back?"

"Did you do something to the guys?" Eva
asked suspiciously.

"You mean, did we sink their canoe or something?" Katie asked as my friends walked over
to the barbecue. "Believe it or not, those macho
men are managing to lose all on their own."

"Yeah, we're beating them fair and square,"
Al chimed in.

"No way!" Eva cried, planting her hands on her hips. "There's no way you could be ahead."

"You must have cheated somehow," Stacy agreed.

I looked her square in the face. "You should have more faith in what we women can do when we set our minds to it. Now you're not only a traitor, Stacy. You're about to become a loser, too!"

"Stroke!" I yelled, and the four of us turned our backs in perfect sync and walked away, leaving Stacy and her clones gaping.

We unpacked the food we'd brought and dug in. I don't remember ever being so hungry in my life. I finished the hot dog and then ate a whole tuna sandwich and an orange besides.

We'd almost finished our meal when we heard laughing, raucous voices coming from the river. The boys' canoe came around the bend at a leisurely pace. They were barely paddling.

Stacy, Eva, B.Z., and Laurel ran down to the riverbank to meet them just as the guys started jumping ashore.

"Maybe we should fire that emergency flare," Sam yelled to Greg. "I think the girls' team must have drowned."

All the guys laughed. Then they caught sight of Stacy's grim expression. And *then* they caught sight of us as we were cleaning up the litter from our lunch.

I swear, it was ten full seconds before any of the guys said a word. They just stood there staring. Finally Greg managed to stammer, "H-how did you get here?"

I reached over and picked up one of the University of Minnesota sweatshirts and waved it at him.

His face went dark with anger. "That was you?"

We all nodded.

"That's cheating!" Jason said. "We thought that was a bunch of college guys."

"If we had known it was you . . ." Sam stammered.

Just then Brendan appeared, checking his watch and scribbling on his clipboard. "Eighteen minutes and thirty-five seconds!" he announced. "You dudes are really going to have to paddle to make up for that kind of a lead."

"Eighteen minutes!" Sam exploded. "We can't make up eighteen minutes!"

"Oh, yes, we can," Greg vowed. "They can only trick us once. And they're still pathetic canoers. Remember that practice we video-taped?"

Naturally, we all cracked up. "We faked that," Sabs explained when she'd managed to catch her breath. "We knew you were watching, so we set it all up."

As the truth began to dawn on them, the four guys exchanged looks of pure fear.

"How about that pathetic start?" Greg insisted nervously.

We just grinned back at him.

"They must have waited till we got out of sight," Sam said thoughtfully. "Then they put on the sweatshirts so when they passed us, we wouldn't realize it was them." He gave Sabs a little mock bow. "I have to hand it to you, sis, you girls came up with a very clever plan. It's so sneaky, I wish I'd thought of it myself."

But Greg wasn't about to take it so lightly. "I'm not going to go around school being humiliated just because a bunch of girls tricked us."

I held up my wrist and pointed to my watch. "Eighteen minutes. That's how long you have to wait here until you can start after us. Maybe you're still a little stronger than we are, and a little bit faster, but you're not eighteen minutes faster."

"This was *supposed* to be an athletic contest," Stacy said, rushing to Greg's side. "Not a contest of . . . of . . ."

"Brains?" Katie offered. "See, that's where you're wrong, Stace. A really good athlete has to be a *smart* athlete, too. Every sport involves intelligence and strategy and planning, as well as muscles."

"Yeah, well, two can play that game," Greg said bitterly. Then he turned and stormed away. Sam and the other guys just sort of shrugged good-naturedly and followed after him.

"I don't think Greg is taking this very well," Al observed dryly.

We rested a while longer, then sauntered back down to the canoe.

"You girls taking off?" Brendan asked, following us down to the water.

"Yes," I said. "We're ready."

"Okay, I'll start the timer as soon as you shove off. Then, eighteen minutes and thirty-five seconds later, I'll let the boys go."

I nodded. "Cool."

"Now, don't forget what I told you about that little sandbar a mile downstream. Go around it to the left."

"Thanks, Brendan," I said.

We piled into our canoe and settled into our seats. "Ready?" I asked.

"Ready!" everyone shouted.

"Then stroke!"

We took off at a good rate of speed, heading for the fastest part of the current. I glanced back and saw the guys watching us intently.

We paddled along nicely, making good time. Allison checked her watch regularly.

"Okay, that's eighteen minutes," she announced. "The guys should be starting out just about now."

"No problem," Katie said confidently. "We're miles ahead."

"Yeah, but we can't let up," I warned.

"Hey, my feet are all wet," Sabs complained.

"We're in a boat," Katie replied. "What do you expect?"

"No, wait! My feet are wet, too. I mean, *really* wet," Al cried. "There's water in the bottom of the boat!"

I looked down. Sure enough, there was at least an inch of water in the boat. "This never happened before," I said.

"It's getting deeper!" Sabs moaned.

"She's right, Randy!" Al confirmed. "We're sinking!"

In the twenty seconds I'd been watching, the water had risen another inch. In a few minutes, I knew, the whole canoe would be swamped.

"What should we do?" Katie asked, still sounding fairly calm.

"Look! Up ahead." Sabs pointed. "It's that sandbar."

"Paddle," I yelled. "Head straight for the sandbar!"

We all started paddling furiously as the water rose over our ankles. Unfortunately, the extra weight of the water slowed us down. Soon the water in the boat was half a foot deep.

Suddenly we felt the canoe grind on the sandy bottom. I looked over the side and saw, to my relief, that we had finally reached the edge of the sandbar.

"Everyone out," I instructed. "We have to

drag the canoe up onto the sandbar."

We all jumped out, and I felt my feet sink into the cold, wet sand. It was hard to drag the canoe up, since it was full of water and weighed a ton, but we finally managed to get it up onto dry sand. Of course, we were a long way from shore, with water rushing all around us on all sides, but at least we weren't sinking.

"Let's turn it over and dump out the water," Allison suggested.

That turned out to be harder than it sounded. But after several attempts, we finally managed to tip the canoe over and empty out the water.

"Hey!" Sabs called out. "Look what I found!"

I rushed over to see what she was pointing at. There, right in the middle of the bottom, was a small hole, about as big around as my thumb.

"It looks like someone drilled that hole!" Katie said angrily. "Look how neat it is."

Al ran her finger around the hole. "There's still something gummy here. I bet whoever drilled the hole put something sticky in the hole to plug it up temporarily. Some chewing gum, maybe. Once we had the canoe out on the water, the plug slowly dissolved or came off and the hole opened."

"Very clever," I said. "I'll bet it was Stacy."

"I'll bet it was Greg," Katie countered.

"I'm sure it wasn't Sam," Sabs said defensively. "He wants to win, but he would never cheat like this."

"Well, whoever did it, we're in trouble now," I said angrily.

"We don't have any way of repairing it." Katie flopped down onto the sand. "This is so bogus."

I looked around helplessly. All we had in the boat was leftover food and our sweatshirts and caps. And Sabs's portable beauty salon!

I jumped over Katie and pounced on the knapsack.

"This is a strange time to be worrying about your looks," Sabs said. "Even I don't care how I look right now."

I was too busy tearing through all the bottles and pins and assorted junk to answer.

"Hey! Careful where you're throwing all that stuff!" Sabs protested.

"Aha!" I cried, holding up Sabs's hairbrush

with a triumphant smile.

Suddenly Al leaped to her feet. "Look! It's the guys!"

We all gazed upstream in horror. Sure enough, the guys' canoe was heading toward us at a good speed.

"Quick!" I shouted. There was no time to lose. "Get ready!"

"But we have a hole in our canoe!" Al said.

I ran to the canoe and reached inside. The hole was a little too small, but I shoved hard and an instant later the handle of Sabs's hairbrush jammed into the hole.

"Not anymore we don't," I yelled.

Everyone sprang into action, lifting the canoe and racing toward the water's edge. We jumped in, just as the boys' team was drawing even with us.

"Stroke!" I yelled, and our canoe began to move, slicing into the current. The guys were still behind us by about ten feet.

We laid into it with all our strength, hoping all our practice could still pay off.

As we rounded a bend in the river, the finish line was visible a few hundred feet away. Across the river, someone had strung a big red banner marked FINISH. On both banks kids waved signs and shouted encouragement.

The guys were gaining on us, but only very slowly, a few inches at a time, and the finish line was growing closer by the moment.

We paddled till I thought my arms would fall off, but still the guys were drawing closer. Out of the corner of my eye, I could see that the front of their canoe was even with the back of ours. Katie could have reached out and touched their boat, if she'd wanted to.

"Stroke!" I yelled hoarsely.

Our paddles sliced through the water and we practically flew. But the guys were on us, drawing closer and closer by the moment.

Then I heard a cheer go up from the crowd as the finish line flashed past.

The race was over. I could hardly believe it. We had won!

Chapter Ten

On Monday morning I took a deep breath and tightened my grip on the bag I was carrying. "So, you guys ready?" I asked as we stood outside the doors to the school.

"I'm ready," Sabs said, nodding her head quickly.

"I'm sure this will be an educational experience," Al added.

"I think I can deal with it," Katie offered.

"Now, we want to be fair, right?" I said. "I mean, just because we won — just because we slaughtered them — doesn't mean we should try and humiliate all the people who bet against us, right?"

Sabs, Katie, and Al all looked at me skeptically.

"On the other hand . . ." I said, grinning.

"On the other hand, let us not forget the Four Stooges jokes," Katie pointed out.

"And let's not forget all that 'weaker sex' stuff," Sabs said.

Allison shook her head regretfully. "I'm afraid we are just going to have to humiliate the guys — for their own good, of course. I mean, they have to learn."

"Oh, yes, absolutely for their own good," I agreed.

"It's not that we *want* to humiliate them," Sabs said, giggling a little, "it's our *obligation* to do it."

"It's sort of a sacred duty," Katie said.

I sighed again. "Well, if we *must* ... "

We pushed open the doors and marched inside. The first person we saw was Scottie Silver. He muttered something under his breath and quickly turned away.

"Excuse me, Scottie!" Katie called out.

Scottie stopped in his tracks and groaned. "Are you really going to make me do this, Katie?"

"You made the bet," she pointed out.

He shook his head in defeat. "Oh, all right. All hail the mighty girls' team," he sort of mumbled.

"I can't hear you," Katie said, with her hands

on her hips. "The bet was that you would *shout* it whenever you saw me. I don't call that a shout."

"All hail the mighty girls' team!" Scottie shouted.

Just then Arizonna came cruising up. Of course, I had to blink twice to be sure it was him.

"That *is* you, isn't it?" I asked doubtfully.

"Hey, I pay off on my bets, babe," Arizonna said, grinning good-naturedly. "How do you like the new look? I had to borrow the clothes from my dad."

"Cool," I said, suppressing a laugh. Arizonna, who normally thinks surfer shorts are formal wear, was dressed in a three-piece navy-blue pin-striped business suit and black oxford shoes.

He twirled around to show me the whole outfit. "Poor dude," he added. "My dad thinks I've like changed permanently. I haven't seen him this happy since I brought home a B in history."

"All hail the mighty girls' team!" Scottie shouted again. "How many more times do I have to —"

"Until I've had enough," Katie said.

"Hey, Zone," I asked Arizonna, "have you seen Greg or Sam? Or Stacy?"

"No way." He laughed. "But I am looking forward to that."

We proceeded down the hallway toward our lockers, still being followed by Scottie, who yelled out his "all hail" message every few seconds. It was like having our own traveling announcer wherever we went.

Three more guys passed by and, on a look from Al, grudgingly bowed low before us. Then they straightened up, twirled around three times, and recited "I'm a Little Teapot."

"Good bet, Al," I commented. "I like it."

"Thanks," she said as we continued to stroll along like conquering heroes.

When Winslow Barton passed us on the way to his own locker, he ran over to ceremoniously hand Sabs a box of doughnuts and sing the theme song from "The Beverly Hillbillies."

"The doughnuts were a nice touch," I complimented Sabs. "But why 'The Beverly Hillbillies' music?"

Sabs shrugged. "It was the only song he knew. If I'd lost the bet, I would have had to sing that song from *Annie*. You know, the one about the sun coming up tomorrow?"

I cringed. "I hate that song. It's a good thing we won."

Now, I have to admit, it was fun cruising down the hallway being followed by a guy singing the beginning of "The Beverly Hillbillies" theme song, but I wanted more. I wanted the four guys on the team. And then I wanted Stacy "The Traitor" Hansen.

When we got to our lockers, we saw them. The boys' team — at last!

We just stood there and stared. There they were, our defeated enemies.

"Nice," I said finally.

Greg, Sam, Nick, and Jason were wearing T-shirts with the words SPORTS WIMP across the front. But that was only the beginning of their fashion statement. They all were wearing plaid shorts, dark dress socks, and sandals. Basically, they couldn't have looked like bigger dweebs if they'd tried.

But, of course, there was also the hair.

I went up to Greg and touched the heavily moussed spike of hair that stuck up from his head like the peak on a soft-serve ice-cream cone. "Very impressive," I commented approvingly.

"On some people, those outfits would look too — well, just *too*," Sabs said, eyeing them critically. "But somehow you guys manage to pull it off."

"Go ahead, gloat," Sam muttered.

"By the way, Sam," Sabs said sweetly, "when you made my bed this morning, you forgot to fluff my pillow." She looked at me and grinned. "I just hate an unfluffed pillow, don't you?"

"By the way, Nick," Al said, "what are you serving us for lunch today?"

"Roast beef or turkey sandwiches," Nick mumbled. "Coleslaw and potato chips."

"And for dessert?" Katie asked.

"Brownies or apple pie," Jason said.

"Not a bad menu," I said. "And being waited on in front of the whole cafeteria should be fun, too."

"You know, I actually thought you girls might be nice about all this, but you're really going to rub it in, aren't you?" Greg muttered.

"Why shouldn't we?" I snapped. "After the way you guys cheated."

"Cheated?" Jason echoed. "We did not!"

"Oh, I suppose that hole just accidentally

got drilled in our canoe?" I said.

"Whoa, that wasn't us!" Sam said, looking serious. Or at least as serious as he could look, under the circumstances.

"No way," Greg agreed. "We wanted to win, but there's no way we'd cheat like that."

I looked at him closely. "Are you telling me you guys honestly didn't make that hole?"

"Cross my heart," Greg said, making a crossing gesture over the words SPORTS WIMP on his shirt.

"Then who —?" But suddenly I realized who.

Al figured it out at the same instant. We looked at each other and said, "Stacy!"

"That could be," Nick said helpfully. "I saw her down by your canoe while we were eating lunch."

I can't say I was surprised. Stacy is a pro at underhanded stunts. Besides, now that I thought about it, it would have been strange for Sam to allow his teammates to sabotage his own sister's boat. Sabs and Sam may hate each other, but not as much as they love each other.

"Time to go find Stacy," Katie said, setting her jaw in a determined way.

"Sorry I accused you of cheating," I told the four guys.

"Does this mean you'll let us off the hook on all these bets?" Sam asked hopefully.

I laughed. "Nice try, but no way."

"Not a chance," Sabs agreed.

We headed off down the hall, still followed by our chorus of singers and shouters. They was starting to get on my nerves a little now, and I realized we'd probably have to let them stop soon — as soon as I was sure they'd suffered enough.

"There!" Katie cried suddenly.

"What?"

"Stacy! I saw her duck into the girls' bathroom!"

"Was she dressed in black leather?" I demanded.

Katie shook her head. "Baby-blue sweater dress."

"Well" — I shook my head regretfully —"that simply *won't* do."

We raced down the hall to the girls' bathroom, leaving our noisy followers behind. Inside we found Stacy, flanked by Eva, B.Z., and Laurel. They looked like cornered rats.

I pointed an accusing finger at Stacy. "You made a bet, Stacy, and now it's time to pay off!"

"I'm not going to!" she cried.

"She's not going to do it!" Eva echoed.

"She doesn't even *own* anything black. Let alone anything leather!" Laurel added.

I lifted the bag I'd been carrying. "Fortunately, I thought of that."

"You can't make me do it," Stacy hissed.

"Oh, but I can," I said sweetly. "You see, I know you're the one who drilled that hole in our canoe."

I was pleased to see her turn a few shades paler.

"And if you don't pay up on your bet, I'm afraid I'll have no choice but to tell our principal that you destroyed someone else's property."

Katie shook her head and made a *tsk-tsk* sound. "How embarrassing for the principal to find out that his own daughter is a cheat."

"And a vandal," Al added. "If he ever knew, he'd probably feel he had to make an example of you."

"He certainly couldn't let you get away with it," Sabs agreed. "That would look like he was playing favorites."

You could almost see the wheels turning in Stacy's head as she thought it over. When her shoulders sagged, I knew we'd won. I tossed her the bag.

She shot me a poisonous look and spun on her heels. She entered one of the stalls, and for the next few minutes all we heard were groans and muttering.

Then, at last, the stall door opened and a whole new Stacy appeared. The baby-blue sweater dress was gone. Instead she wore a black leather jacket, a black T-shirt, a tight black leather miniskirt, and heavy biker boots. Her hair was caught up under a black cap.

"It's the *real* you, Stace," I said in a super-friendly tone. "Honest."

"I'll get you for this, *Rowena*!" she snapped. "Come on," she yelled to Eva, B.Z., and Laurel. "Let's get out of here."

"Um, you go on ahead," Eva said, eyeing Stacy's outfit.

"We'll, uh, catch you later," Laurel agreed.

"I think your clones are bailing out on you," I said, laughing.

Stacy stomped out into the hall, and we followed, while Eva, B.Z., and Laurel slunk away in the opposite direction.

"Well, are you happy now?" Al asked. "We won, we made the entire school pay off their bets, and we actually got Stacy the Great's faithful clones to desert her, if only for a little while."

I nodded in satisfaction. "Yes, it's been a good morning, so far. I can't think of any way I could possibly be happier."

Just then someone yelled, "Hey, Randy! Way to go!"

I looked up and saw this eighth-grade guy waving. Only he wasn't waving at me. He was waving at Stacy.

"I am *not* Randy Zak!" she shouted back, as if he'd just totally insulted her.

"He thought Stacy was you!" Allison said, starting to giggle.

"Well, I was wrong. There *was* a way for me to be even happier."

As we all laughed, Scottie yelled "All hail!" Winslow began another verse of "The Beverly Hillbillies" and several guys broke into one more round of "I'm a Little Teapot."

"Stroke!" I shouted. We linked arms and headed down the hall to first period.

Don't Miss
GIRL TALK #42
ALLISON'S BABY-SITTING ADVENTURE

"All right, everyone," said Ms. Staats, picking up a stack of papers on her desk. "I have all the information about the Give-a-Thon right here. How you raise the money is up to you, of course, but the deadline for the Give-a-Thon is in three weeks, so make sure you register your teams as soon as possible. I should also tell you that —"

Suddenly Stacy raised her hand.

"Oh, Ms. Staats," she called in the sugary voice she uses with teachers and other grown-ups .she wants to impress.

"Yes, Stacy?" said Ms. Staats, looking up from her papers.

"Ms. Staats, I'd like to be the first in our class to volunteer for this worthy cause."

I glanced at Randy, who rolled her eyes. I knew she was thinking the same thing I was thinking — Stacy always has to be the first to do anything in our class. She thinks it makes her special or something.

"Well, that's fine, Stacy," said Ms. Staats. "But

you can't register on your own, you know. You'll need to form a team."

"Oh, that's no problem," said Stacy brightly. "Eva Malone, B. Z. Latimer, and Laurel Spencer are all going to be on my team, too."

I couldn't help noticing that Eva, B.Z., and Laurel looked pretty surprised when Stacy said this. After all, there hadn't been any time for them to think about whether they *wanted* to volunteer or not.

"Okay, girls, that's fine," said Ms. Staats, writing in their names on the form in front of her.

I glanced at Randy, Sabs, and Katie. I definitely thought Magic Star sounded like a pretty cool organization, and I wondered if they would be willing to volunteer for this thing. I caught Randy's eye again, and she gave me the thumbs-up sign, nudging Sabrina with her other arm. As Sabs and Katie turned to look at me, I raised my eyebrows, and they both nodded immediately. It still amazed me that my friends and I could have an entire conversation without saying one word.

TALK BACK!
TELL US WHAT YOU THINK ABOUT GIRL TALK BOOKS

Name _____

Address _____

City _____ State _____ Zip_____

Birthday _____ Mo._____ Year _____

Telephone Number (____)_____

1) Did you like this GIRL TALK book?

Check one: YES_____ NO_____

2) Would you buy another GIRL TALK book?

Check one: YES_____ NO_____

If you like GIRL TALK books, please answer questions 3-5;
otherwise go directly to question 6.

3) What do you like most about GIRL TALK books?

Check one: Characters_____ Situations_____
         Telephone Talk_____Other_____

4) Who is your favorite GIRL TALK character?

Check one: Sabrina_____ Katie_____ Randy_____
Allison_____ Stacy_____ Other (give name) _____

5) Who is your *least* favorite character?

_____

6) Where did you buy this GIRL TALK book?

Check one: Bookstore____Toy store____Discount store____
Grocery store___Supermarket___Other (give name)_____

Please turn over to continue survey.

7) How many GIRL TALK books have you read?

Check one: 0_____   1 to 2_____   3 to 4 _____   5 or more_____

8) In what type of store would you look for GIRL TALK books?

Bookstore_____Toy store_____Discount store_____

Grocery store_____Supermarket_____Other (give name)_____

9) Which type of store would you visit most often if you wanted to buy a GIRL TALK book?

Check *only* one: Bookstore_____Toy store_____

Discount store_____Grocery store_____Supermarket_____

Other (give name)_____

10) How many books do you read in a month?

Check one: 0_____   1 to 2_____   3 to 4 _____   5 or more_____

11) Do you read any of these books?
Check those you have read:

The Baby-sitters Club_____ Nancy Drew_____

Pen Pals_____ Sweet Valley High _____

Sweet Valley Twins_____Gymnasts_____

12) Where do you shop most often to buy these books?

Check one: Bookstore_____Toy store_____

Discount store_____Grocery store_____Supermarket_____

Other (give name)_____

13) What other kinds of books do you read most often?

_____

14) What would you like to read more about in GIRL TALK?

_____

_____

Send completed form to :
GIRL TALK Survey, Western Publishing Company, Inc.
1220 Mound Avenue, Mail Station #85
Racine, Wisconsin 53404

LOOK FOR THE AWESOME GIRL TALK BOOKS IN A STORE NEAR YOU!

Fiction

MORE GIRL TALK TITLES TO LOOK FOR

Nonfiction
ASK ALLIE 101 answers to your questions about boys, friends, family, and school!

YOUR PERSONALITY QUIZ Fun, easy quizzes to help you discover the real you!

BOYTALK: HOW TO TALK TO YOUR FAVORITE GUY